Betelgeuse Dimming

Betelgeuse Dimming

Jean-Paul L. Garnier

SPACE COWBOY BOOKS

SPACE COWBOY BOOKS
61871 Twentynine Palms Hwy.
Joshua Tree, CA 92252
www.spacecowboybooks.com

Betelgeuse Dimming
ISBN# 978-1-7328257-3-4

First Edition | 2020
Cover art by Zara Kand
Book design by Jon Christopher

Introduction

When I first heard news of Betelgeuse dimming and potentially going nova within my lifetime it filled me with tremendous excitement. Every night I would go outside to look at the sky and hope that I would have the privilege of seeing our sky lit up with the splendor of a relatively nearby stellar explosion. While stars are exploding throughout the universe on a regular basis it is a rare occurrence that we might see one with the naked eye. If Betelgeuse were to explode it would be a jewel in the night sky for weeks and be visible during the day, nearly as bright as our sun. This excitement brought me out to the yard night after night in hopes of seeing the show, but at the same time it filled me with an immense guilt. The guilt I felt was the flipside of my prayers to witness the stellar death, because in all likelihood there are planets orbiting that star, and if there are planets then there is potentially life. If Betelgeuse were to go nova it would mean the end of any civilization that may be living in proximity of the star. Not just the planets around the star but also planets within range of the powerful cosmic rays that the explosion would unleash. While I hoped to see the nova I realized that I was also reveling in the potential demise of multiple civilizations and while this would have occurred centuries ago it couldn't be right for me to wish it so. All throughout my excitement this guilt plagued me, right up until it was announced that the star's dimming was part of a regular stellar cycle and that the star in all likelihood would not go nova for millennia to come. When this announcement was made I was half way through writing the poem *Betelgeuse Dimming* and at once felt a wave of relief for the people that the nova would have possibly destroyed and a sadness that I may never have the opportunity to see a nova with my own eyes. It seemed for a moment that the relevance of this poem would be moot since the nova was not imminent but I realized that the feelings that came up for me those nights of watching the winter wanderer pass by were still powerful, for if life is common in the universe then so is the frequent destruction of many of those possible civilizations. Such is the cycle of the cosmos' potentiality coming into expression only to be wiped out and become the seeds of the next potential. In many ways I'm glad that Betelgeuse will remain intact, but I still yearn for the beauty of a nova in my lifetime.

The three other poems in this collection also share the theme of space, a regular obsession of mine. *Flight Notes* is a series of haiku that tells the tale of a colonization mission and their perils. *Last Contact* is about the probable inability to communicate with another species and their subsequent departure. And lastly, *Sky Burial* is about the soul being trapped in the body when the remains are frozen in the vacuum. While *Betelgeuse Dimming* is technically a science poem, the rest of the collection is purely science fiction.

It was with great pleasure that I was able to record this book as an album with two of my close friends – RedBlueBlackSilver and Field Collapse. We got together at Joshua Tree Art & Music and laid the tracks down live with improvised music. I love the intrinsic relationship between poetry and music and am ever grateful to my pals for understanding my work so well that they nail it every time.

Jean-Paul L. Garnier
Joshua Tree, 2020

Contents

Introduction 5

Betelgeuse Dimming 9

Flight Notes 23

Last Contact 27

Sky Burial 31

Bios 35

Betelgeuse Dimming

receiving word of your imminent nova
we await the neutrino flood
signaling your demise
as you dim before us
before in time
future colors paint our minds
*

the night holds new treasures
our constellations change
evenings spent waiting for you to vanish
in kaleidoscopic majesty
centuries of wait
our telescopes trained
*

praying for explosions
tears taint my wonder
thinking of your culture lost
in the fiery display
flowers in our sky
shines with our sun briefly
*

materials of life
stripped away so many centuries ago
reduced to headlines
lacking all essence
of your unknowable ways
the arts we will never see
*

the way of all stars
takes you before my birth
weeks of light
temporary remains, we may have spoken
we, teething still
during your renaissance
*

now we listen and see
the wake of your silence
without having met, we mourn
nightly, lament the distances
from your star flee
may we meet yet
*

were you breaking rocks
when telescopes could have warned
the spacefaring know
still gravity hinders
home becomes burning prison
amidst cosmic splendor
*

were you witness
to others, feel the same way
beg the contact
which could never come
great voids
only growing, slowly growing
*

if I mourn, as I do early evenings
it is too late for worth
your perish ancient
fresh
cosmic rays hold no detail
lost in the noise forever
*

no more shall you redden the sky
small point of miracle
punctuating the winter wanderer
in endless pursuit
now forgotten your myths
of which we were but a pin-prick of light
*

watching you fade
billions may have fallen
so many stories
dust sails on the medium
we may have loved each other
or only misunderstood
*

dimming, still dimming
only noticing after being told
as if trivial the many
the multitude wiped away
looking, still looking
fearfully excited
*

anticipation rise, stomach drop
your photons arrive alone
carrierless and random
seeking the coherence
again sadness
that times seldom align
*

signaling us pre-birth
only aware of visible light in the trees
you thought us non-existent
building our antennae
long after signals pass
deaf planets
*

warm tears quickly cool
following the wanderer
blurring the faint point
to nothing before its time
before the show of fire
before the end
*

what signs pointed
fingers outstretched toward oblivion
peering into the expansion
as flame nears
atmospheres cast off
seas join sky
*

a sky blacker without you
larger void
may your rays ignite
new material for life
may they stir clouds
into order
*

dust cloud to dust cloud
memories gone before accretion
energies swirl
will they carry our past
in shrinking ovals
until it may speak again
*

the light still travels
eternal, dissipating
wanting to be noticed
forever leaving the source
forever containing wisdom and folly
undeciphered by us, for now
*

I wish my eye was planets wide
reading entire spectrum
comprehending all forms
blazing information
memories of every sentience
working the waves
*

the same moistened eye
moved by the opposite of desire
limited in ways
you could have shown us
uncommon frames of reference
potentially so useful
*

those centuries ago
holding each other in the knowing
those who could not escape
terrible knowledge
forewarned apocalypse
or blissfully naïve in the caves
*

or in the caves survive
waiting for the air to mix the vacuum
a slower death
instant winds of fire
preferable unless needing
time for prayer
*

nightly guilt descends
pleasure grimace
of beautiful doom
wincing as I remember you
circled the dying star
when it was life-giver
*

all suns – infanticide
the time of cleansing
bitter rebirth
temperatures of fusion
matter now joining
burning generations
*

spewing gold which may never arrive
omnidirectional color, heat
warming lovely shores no more
no more tanning lovely skins
pelt or leaves
evaporating towards heaven
*

the beautiful coming apart
my future, your past
we, never to share a present
the meaninglessness of now
a now which never comes
now the wanting last
*

who watches, thinks these thoughts
as our parent swallows her children
perhaps another trite old song
the common lament
echoed through the cosmos
reiterated so many times
*

implosions infinite
constants still constant
nuclear dance while all spin
pirouette of creation
awareness the rarity
and now one less
*

one more to reach its end
rotting on the vine or venturing
toward us or away
may new soil move
beneath your extremities
may new seas part with your stroke
*

your red pallor
vague ecliptical memories
grace mornings
each night may be the last
when you sail our skies
unhindered by destruction
*

after fading
fading from my mind within weeks
guilt reduced to eulogies
teach me to sing
your songs vanished forever
songs of your people
*

we lacked the time
for images of you
only now seeing the possibilities
of a connection never made
if you had waited
if you had a choice
*

please send one final burst
archives reaching through space
collections of knowledge
spilling through stars
open arms await
the histories of your achievement
*

receiving news of false alarm
klaxon of the mind
falters in disbelief
still, our deaths lurk
around every shining sphere
truths relative – bending light
*

your convectious view
roiling in polished glass
ripples through academies
whose secrets public cannot fathom
not held hostage
yet amplified through technicalities
*

our mistake repeatable
always so sure
in the churning universe
certainties are flawed
and death will come
surely as the sun may not rise
*

even if not within my life
someone witness
the countless deaths
on every glowing horizon
the stellar sway
predetermined and beautiful
*

ghastly predictable beauty
cosmic dialectic
the creator's pendulum
slants in entropy's favor
cannot truly keep time
throughout infinity
*

time sped up
a fireworks show for the all seeing eye
the all deaf ear
or one who listens
remaining silent keeping record
for the book of time's end
*

and all this heat
dies cold and isolated
when once light peppered
the terrible backdrop
of endless voids
placed there by fluctuations
*

receiving word of your imminent nova
all await the neutrino flood
signaling possible demise
as you brighten before us
at one time
future colors painted our thoughts

Flight Notes

this intense rumble
last but one earth minute
yet sends me through space

now my first earthrise
startling, fearsome and still
fragile perspective

spacecraft passes plume
photographs rare occurrence
begs many questions

mighty wind from sun
shaping the sky into dance
colors of heaven

dew, helmet, condense
filter system not working
damn the engineers

the airlock opens
vacuum welcomes open void
loneliness of space

the very first step
the planet was a virgin
trodden from now on

soil beneath boot
for all perhaps a great step
though cold is the ground

projectile comes forth
into ancient snowball
hammer of knowledge

so months disappear
into training for the night
which we shall travel

Last
Contact

as they left I heard cheering
unsure if it was mixed with tears
or was it shouting, begging
we never crossed the language barrier
protestors held signs scrawled with equations
even these symbol sets
remained a mystery

it shook its head and turned away
rejoining its crew
for departure
for us it meant no
it could have meant anything
body language meaningless
we could have shaken the wrong extremity

they leave on a pillar of fire
smoke signal of farewell
a burnt patch of earth
monument to the failure of our linguists
knowing less than before, abandoned
they said something before they left
but I could not hear it through the cheering

Sky
Burial

our first sky burial was today
frozen, traveling forever
she would have wanted it this way
as she left for the stars
we cried for arriving
a comet now
gone to heaven
*

bodies meant to deteriorate
freeing the energy
vacating the dimension
frozen, traveling forever
static zero, absolute soul
void calling
cold impersonal open arms of God
*

a tunnel of darkness
nothing like the reports
one cannot leave when they have already left
I could hear their voices
viewed from above
I begged not to be sent to the void
yet human sadness needs remains gone
*

with diminished crew spirits plummet
stars become graveyard
infinitude populated with loss
we see her as a star
and now they all look the same
will she travel the forever
or join with Sun
*

transmutation ends with cold
spirits break entropy if freed from mass
or time can stop as your light is trapped
the containment field entered from the void
frozen, traveling forever
meant to let go
caged through sky burial
*

may Suns call to me
I would grow to draw them in
perhaps consciousness could if freed
bodies meant to deteriorate
as a vapor I could move
taking their sorrow with me
as I leave all stars to become only one
*

Jean-Paul L. Garnier lives and writes in Joshua Tree, CA where he is the owner of Space Cowboy Books, a science fiction bookstore, independent publisher, and producer of *Simultaneous Times* podcast. In 2020 his first novella *Garbage In, Gospel Out* was released by Space Cowboy Books and in 2018 Traveling Shoes Press released *Echo of Creation*, a collection of his science fiction short stories. He has also released several collections of poetry: *In Iudicio* (Cholla Needles Press 2017) and *Future Anthropology* (Space Cowboy Books 2019) which was nominated for the Elgin Award. His short stories, poetry, and essays have appeared in many anthologies and webzines.

http://jplgarnier.blogspot.com/

RedBlueBlackSilver is a multi-instrumentalist based in Joshua Tree, CA specializing in creating music for film and podcasts. You can hear his music regularly on *Space Cowboy Books Presents Simultaneous Times* and *Desert Oracle Radio*. His documentary film work includes the soundtrack to *Hunt for the Skinwalker*, and his music also appears in *Bob Lazar: Area 51 & Flying Saucers* (both directed by Jeremy Kenyon Lockyer Corbell).

https://redblueblacksilver.com/

Field Collapse is an electronic music collective based out of Joshua Tree, CA. It is led by composer and experimental musical instrument builder Dain Luscombe. You can hear their music regularly in the *Simultaneous Times* Podcast and television shows such as *Altered Carbon, Mythbusters* and the *White Rabbit Project*.

https://lessbells.bandcamp.com/

Other Books by Jean-Paul L. Garnier

Garbage In, Gospel Out - Space Cowboy Books
Future Anthropology - Space Cowboy Books
Echo of Creation - Traveling Shoes Press
In Iudicio - Cholla Needles Press

This book is also available as a free digital album with music by **RedBlueBlackSilver** and **Field Collapse**, recorded live at Joshua Tree Art & Music. The download comes with an ebook version of the book.

Get it free here:

spacecowboybooks.bandcamp.com/album/betelgeuse-dimming

www.ingramcontent.com/pod-product-compliance
Lightning Source LLC
Chambersburg PA
CBHW030543180626
46810CB00005B/1988